Manny the Lamb

Rick Lancaster

with Delores Kight

Illustrated by Dave O'Connell

ISBN: 978-1-945976-04-9

Published by EABooks Publishing, a division of

Living Parables of Central Florida, Inc. a 501c3.

EABooksPublishing.com

In memory of Rick Lancaster,
who created *Manny the Lamb*.

- D.K.

"If a man has one hundred sheep, and one of them
goes astray, doesn't he leave the ninety-nine, go to the
mountains, and seek that which has gone astray? If
he finds it, most certainly I tell you, he rejoices over it
more than over the ninety-nine which have not gone
astray " (Matthew 18:12-13 WEB).

A long time ago, in a pasture far away, lived a lamb named Manny. Manny belonged to Shepherd Jessie who had lots of lambs and sheep. Shepherd Jessie loved and cared for each one.

One day, Manny watched as Shepherd Jessie fixed part of the stone fence that protected the sheep from wild animals. Jessie and his helper lifted large stones and placed them on top of each other to replace the ones that had fallen.

"I'm going to fix the fence today," Jessie told the sheep. "Don't wander through the openings or you might get lost."

"*Baa,*" said Manny. That's the sound sheep make when they talk to people.

Soon, Manny's friend Joy came up beside him.
"Wanna play?" she asked.

"Sure," said Manny.

Manny and Joy ran and jumped and chased each other.

After a while, Manny and Joy ended up near another part of the wall where stones had tumbled down, leaving a hole just the right size for little lambs to squeeze through.

Manny looked at the opening. "Let's taste the grass over there," he said.

"Shepherd Jessie told us not to go past the fence," said Joy. "We need to go back."

Manny stared at the grass on the other side.

"I'll just taste it," Manny said. Then, he squeezed through the opening.

Manny nibbled some of the grass. "Yum. This is delicious! You should come and try it, Joy."

Joy stood firm. "No, Manny. You need to come back."

"I'll eat just a little longer," Manny said. "This grass tastes so good, I don't want to stop eating."

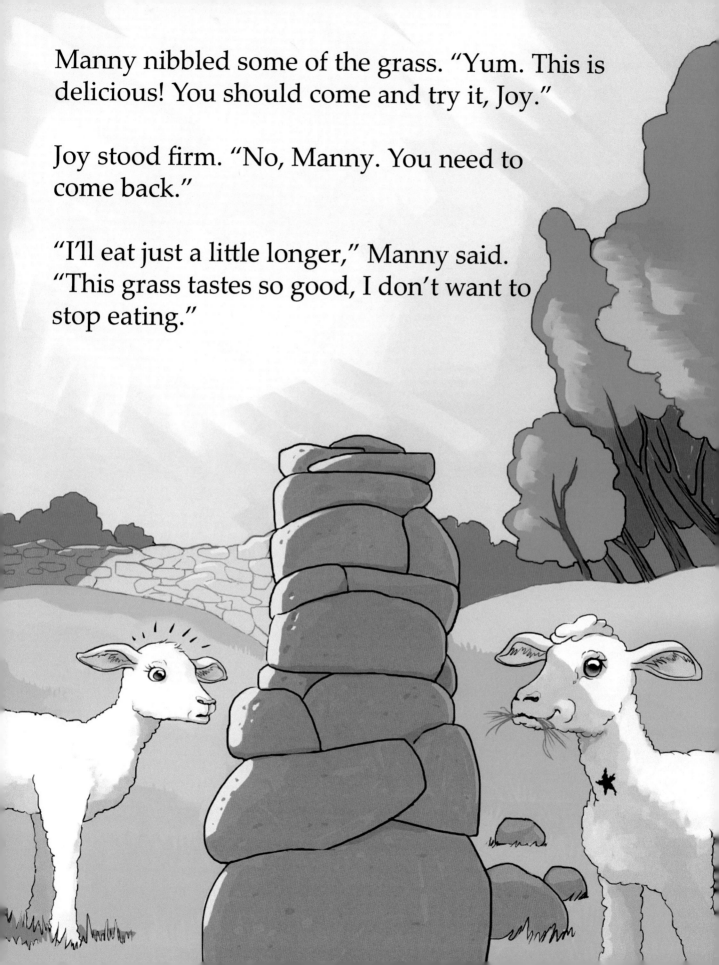

Manny walked farther and nibbled some more. When he turned his head and looked back, he could still see Joy. "I know my way home," he thought. "I'll eat just a little more."

Soon, Manny came to the bottom of a hill. He looked back and saw Joy, so he turned around and walked up the hill, eating more grass along the way.

When he reached the top of the hill, Manny looked back again. "Joy is still there, so I can find my way home," he thought. He was starting to get full, but he nibbled more of the delicious grass as he walked down the other side of the hill.

Manny saw a clear brook. He was thirsty, so he took a long drink of the cool water.

Manny knew it was time to go home. He looked around, but he could not see Joy or the stone fence. He did not know which way to go. "How do I get home?" he cried.

Manny looked to the left and then to the right. He looked in front of him and behind him. "I don't know where I am," he said.

Swish. Swoosh. Branches rustled in a nearby bush.

"What's that?" Manny cried out. "Is it a lion? Shepherd Jessie always chases away the wild animals. I wish he were here to protect me."

A deer leaped out from between the
bushes and ran away.

"Whew," Manny said. "It's only a deer."

"Hoo Hoo!" came from a tree branch.

Manny jumped. "What's that?" he cried out.
"Is it a hawk?"

An owl swooped down from the tree, and then flew up into the sky.

"Whew," Manny said. "It's only an owl."

By now, Manny was tired. He wanted to lie down and go to sleep, but he was too afraid. The sun went lower and lower in the sky. "I wish I had listened to Shepherd Jessie," Manny thought.

The sun disappeared, and the air got cold. Manny shivered. "I miss my friends. We always stay close to each other to keep warm." Finally, Manny lay down. Even though he couldn't see very far in the darkness, he kept his eyes wide open.

Suddenly, Manny heard noises in the nearby bushes. The sounds came closer to him.

Manny jumped up and looked all around. "What's that?"

Just then, Manny saw
Shepherd Jessie
walking toward him.

When Jessie got near, he knelt down next to Manny. "I finally found you, my little lost lamb," the shepherd said in his gentle voice.

Jessie lifted Manny onto his big, strong shoulders. "Now, let me take you home."

Manny was so glad
Shepherd Jessie found him.

As Manny rested on Jessie's shoulders for the trip home, he thought, "I'll never wander away again."

Rick Lancaster attended Southwestern Baptist Theological Seminary, with an emphasis on youth ministry. He ultimately decided on a career in the computer technology field; however, he always kept his love for God and the ministry in his heart. In his IT jobs, he helped to set up computer systems and troubleshoot computer problems. At church, he taught children in Sunday School and played drums in the praise team. After his death in 2017, he continued to bless others by leaving the first draft of *Manny the Lamb*.

After Rick's passing, his mom and dad, Dee and Gerald Lancaster, asked Delores Kight to continue the work on *Manny the Lamb*. Her efforts developed into this children's picture book.

Delores Kight earned a bachelor's degree in journalism from the University of Maryland. Her short stories for children have appeared in *Focus on the Family Clubhouse, Jr., Pockets, Kidz Chat,* and *Power Station* magazines. She has also been published in *The Upper Room* devotional, as well as *Splickety Prime, Christian Communicator,* and *Purpose* magazines. Her love of children led her to teach Sunday School, Junior Church, and Vacation Bible School. An avid attendee at Christian writers conferences, Delores helped cofound and lead the Ocala chapter of Word Weavers International.

Dave O'Connell studied at the College for Creative Studies in Detroit, Michigan. He worked for Skidmore Studio for over 30 years as an illustrator and artist, creating art for many clients like Chevy, Mazda, Ford, Michelin, US Postal, Carfax, and Serta and storyboards for Super Bowl commercials. Dave enjoys taking client scripts to life and seeing them on TV. He has taught art classes at CCS Detroit and McComb College and loves painting and using his art to speak at camps, men's groups, and church youth events. Dave has illustrated and published a spiritual coloring book titled *I Call Him.*

If you and your child(ren) enjoyed reading *Manny the Lamb*, and would like to spread the word about this wholesome children's book, here are some ways you can help:

- Tell your friends;
- Order a copy as a gift;
- Buy a copy for your church's library, day care program, or pre-school;
- Post an online review.

To learn more about *Manny the Lamb*, visit: www.mannythelamb.com.

Made in the USA
Lexington, KY
08 August 2019